W9-BOM-985

THE GREAT PUPPY INVASION

Alastair Heim 🐾 Illustrated by **Kim Smith**

CLARION BOOKS | Houghton Mifflin Harcourt | Boston   New York

CLARION BOOKS
3 Park Avenue, New York, New York 10016

Text copyright © 2017 by Alastair Heim
Illustrations copyright © 2017 by Kim Smith

All rights reserved. For information about permission to
reproduce selections from this book, write to
trade.permissions@hmhco.com or to Permissions,
Houghton Mifflin Harcourt Publishing Company,
3 Park Avenue, 19th Floor, New York, New York 10016.

Clarion Books is an imprint of
Houghton Mifflin Harcourt Publishing Company.

www.hmhco.com

The illustrations in this book were created digitally.
The text was set in Adobe Garamond Pro.
Book design by Sharismar Rodriguez

Library of Congress Cataloging-in-Publication Data
Names: Heim, Alastair, author. | Smith, Kim, 1986– illustrator.
Title: The great puppy invasion / Alastair Heim ; illustrated
by Kim Smith. | Description: Boston ; New York : Clarion
Books, Houghton Mifflin Harcourt, | [2017] | Summary:
When Strictville, where fun, play, and cuteness are all
forbidden, is invaded by hundreds of adorable puppies,
everyone is terrified until Teddy decides to shake the littlest
puppy's paw. | Identifiers: LCCN 2016030315
ISBN 9780544999176 (hardcover) | Subjects:
CYAC: Dogs—Fiction. | Animals—Infancy—Fiction.
City and town life—Fiction. | Humorous stories.
Classification: LCC PZ7.1.H4448 Gre 2017
DDC [E]—dc23 | LC record available at
https://lccn.loc.gov/2016030315

Manufactured in China

SCP 10 9 8 7 6 5 4 3 2 1
4500659495

For Ed Ball . . .
one of this man's best friends
—A.H.

To all the adorable dogs in the dog park
and Whisky, my favorite puppy
—K.S.

One day, a puppy showed up in little Teddy's town.

Then two.

Then hundreds.
The locals panicked. They had never seen puppies before.

Little Teddy's town had a long history of ridiculous rules.

Fun was forbidden.

Play was prohibited.

Cuteness was downright criminal.

And *today* was quickly becoming a colossally . . . cute . . . catastrophe.

The mayor held an emergency meeting in the town hall.
"We must get rid of these adorable creatures," she declared.

The townspeople tried everything they could to rid themselves of the puppies.

They threw sticks at them.

But the puppies brought the sticks right back.

They tried chasing the
puppies away.

But the puppies grew even
more delightful.

"Let's try feeding them," someone suggested.
"THEN maybe they'll leave."

And *that's* when their tails started wagging . . .

What are they doing?

Are they waving at us??

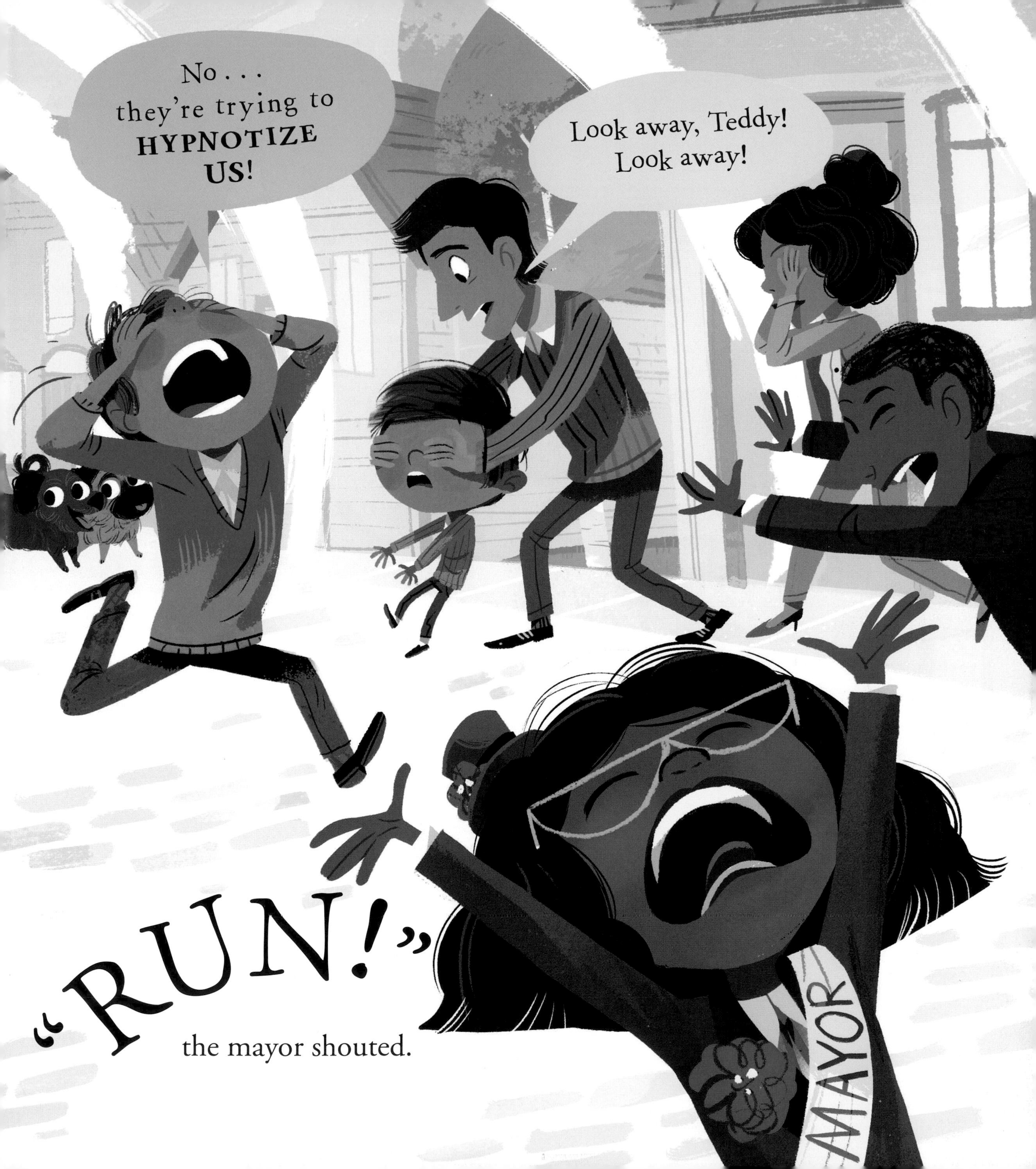

"RUN!"

the mayor shouted.

People ran for their lives!
The puppies trotted along after them.

They **barked**.

They **yip-yipped**.

They **ruff-ruff-ruffed**.

One by one, doors began to slam, slam, slam . . .

. . . until everyone was safely inside.

But, as little Teddy reached his front porch,
he heard a *teeny* whimper . . .
coming from the *tiniest* puppy of all.

And he wondered how something so sweet
and so playful and so adorably sad
could possibly be scary.

Just then, the puppy stepped forward,
sat down on little Teddy's lawn,
and lifted its fuzzy front paw.

Little Teddy approached.
The puppy's enormous eyes grew even larger.

He crept closer and closer
as the townspeople looked on in horror . . .

One by one, the townspeople emerged from their homes.

The rest of the puppies sat down
and lifted their front paws too.

The townspeople cautiously stepped forward,
then carefully crouched down
to kindly shake paws
with the cute, countless canines . . .

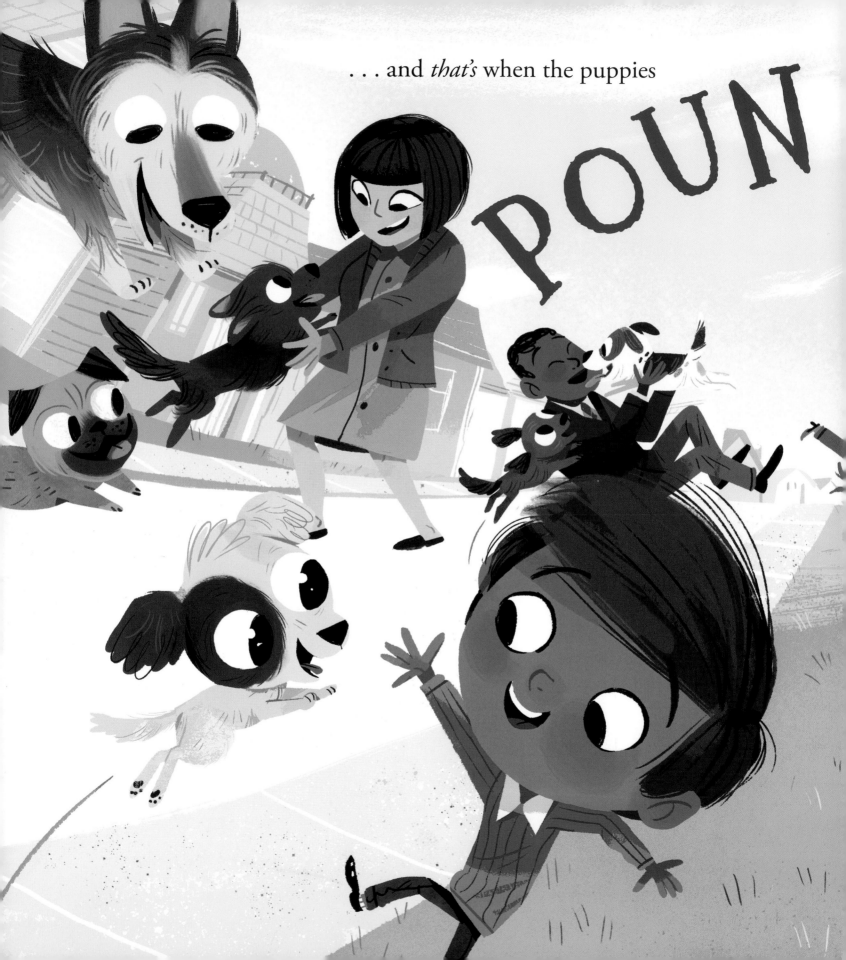

. . . and *that's* when the puppies

POUN

And the townspeople discovered
that they liked puppies after all.

They gave them names.

They taught them tricks.

Some even dressed the puppies
up in silly outfits.

But most important, that day,
the people in little Teddy's town
decided, once and for all . . .

. . . that they would never be afraid of **cuteness** again.

Not So
STRICTVILLE
ALL WORK AND NO PLAY
MAKES FOR A ~~Bad~~ Day!